The Very First THANKSGIVING DAY

by RHONDA GOWLER GREENE

paintings by SUSAN GABER

ALADDIN PAPERBACKS
NEW YORK LONDON TORONTO SYDNEY

For Gary—thanks for all your love and support
—R. G. G.

For Emily
—S. G.

ALADDIN PAPERBACKS
An imprint of Simon & Schuster Children's Publishing Division
1230 Avenue of the Americas, New York, NY 10020
Text copyright © 2002 by Rhonda Gowler Greene
Illustrations copyright © 2002 by Susan Gaber
All rights reserved, including the right of reproduction
in whole or in part in any form.
ALADDIN PAPERBACKS and colophon are
trademarks of Simon & Schuster, Inc.
Also available in an Atheneum Books For Young Readers
hardcover edition.
Designed by Michael Nelson
The text of this book was set in Regula Antiqua.
The illustrations for this book were rendered in acrylic paint.
Manufactured in China
First Aladdin Paperbacks edition October 2006

4 5 6 7 8 9 10

The Library of Congress has cataloged the hardcover edition as follows:
The very first Thanksgiving Day / by Rhonda Gowler Greene ;
illustrated by Susan Gaber—1st ed. p. cm.
Summary: Rhyming verses trace the events leading up to the first
Thanksgiving Day.
1. Thanksgiving Day—Juvenile fiction. [1. Thanksgiving Day—Fiction.
2. Pilgrims (New Plymouth Colony)—Fiction. 3. Stories in rhyme.]
I. Gaber, Susan, ill. II. Title   PZ8.3.G824 Ve 2002
[E]—dc21   00-066387
ISBN-13: 978-0-689-83301-4 (hc.)
ISBN-10: 0-689-83301-6 (hc.)
ISBN-13: 978-1-4169-1916-2 (pbk.)
ISBN-10: 1-4169-1916-3 (pbk.)

AUTHOR'S NOTE

The word "Indian" was used in my text after much consideration. Upon researching, I found that "Indian" is the term preferred by many groups, while "Native American" is preferred by many others. Furthermore, I learned that the Pilgrims used the term "Indian" in their journal entries, which are found in *A Relation or Journal of the Proceedings of the Plantation settled at Plymouth in New England* (London, England, 1622), more commonly know as *Mourt's Relation*. After much thought, I felt the term "Indian" was more fitting for my story. I use it only with the deepest respect. Many thanks to those who helped in this research, including Cynthia Leitich Smith of the Muscogee-Creek Nation, Deborah Stewart, and Ginny Moore Kruse.

The Pilgrims' first harvest feast of 1621, which is thought to have taken place sometime between September 21 and November 9, has become the model for our traditional Thanksgiving Day observance. Fifty-one Pilgrims and at least ninety guests from the Wampanoag tribe were in attendance at this harvest festival, which included feasting and games, and lasted three days.

ILLUSTRATOR'S NOTE

Research for this book has led me to many personal discoveries about the Pilgrims' first year in America. For example, Squanto, a Patuxet Indian, taught the settlers how to successfully plant twenty acres of corn using fish as fertilizer, placing it "spoke-wise" in "hillocks." (The Pilgrims then had to guard their plantings from hungry wolves who would otherwise raid the fields.) Additional food sources included eels, which were plentiful in the Plymouth waters. The Pilgrims would catch them in long baskets (there is a depiction of a boy carrying one on the opposite page), into which the eels would easily enter, but would then have difficulty escaping. Unlike the Puritans in the Massachusetts Bay Colony who wore black, the Pilgrims wore brighter clothing made from cloth or fibers colored by natural dyes produced in Europe or in the Orient. A final interesting discovery was learning that there were two dogs, a spaniel and a mastiff, brought to Plymouth Plantation on the *Mayflower*. It has been these and other revelations about this early time in America's history that has made this project personally rewarding.

This is the very first Thanksgiving Day.

This is the food, gathered and blessed,
the corn and sweet berries, the wild turkey dressed,
shared on the very first Thanksgiving Day.

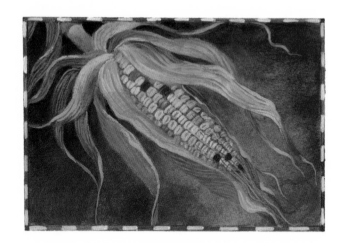

These are the Indians, skillful and strong,
who knew how to live through the winters so long
and ate of the food gathered and blessed.

These are the Pilgrims who farmed the new land,
who steadfastly labored and toiled by hand,
and learned from the Indians, skillful and strong.

These are the houses built in straight rows
that stood in the hot sun and harsh winter snows
and sheltered the Pilgrims who farmed the new land.

This is the harbor marked by a huge stone
where first steps were taken to chart the unknown,
not far from the houses built in straight rows.

This is the *Mayflower* ship in full sail
that weathered the rough seas, the wind and the hail,
and docked in the harbor marked by a huge stone.

This is the ocean that never would end,
that sometimes was foe and sometimes was friend,
that carried the *Mayflower* ship in full sail.

This is the land where it all began,
the land where a brave group made ready their plan
to travel the ocean that never would end,
that sometimes was foe and sometimes was friend,

that carried the *Mayflower* ship in full sail
that weathered the rough seas, the wind and the hail,

and docked in the harbor marked by a huge stone
where first steps were taken to chart the unknown,

not far from the houses built in straight rows
that stood in the hot sun and harsh winter snows

and sheltered the Pilgrims who farmed the new land,
who steadfastly labored and toiled by hand,

and learned from the Indians, skillful and strong,
who knew how to live through the winters so long

and ate of the food, gathered and blessed,
the corn and sweet berries, the wild turkey dressed,

shared on the very first Thanksgiving Day.